SKELLY
the Skeleton Girl

SIMON & SCHUSTER BOOKS FOR YOUNG READERS

An imprint of Simon & Schuster Children's Publishing Division

1230 Avenue of the Americas, New York, New York 10020

Copyright © 2007 by Jimmy Pickering

SIMON & SCHUSTER BOOKS FOR YOUNG READERS is a trademark of Simon & Schuster, Inc.

Book design by Lizzy Bromley

The text for this book is set in Stanyan.

The art for this book was created using mixed media.

Manufactured in China

10 9 8 7 6 5 4 3 2 1

Library of Congress Cataloging-in-Publication Data

Pickering, Jimmy.

Skelly the skeleton girl / Jimmy Pickering.—1st ed.

p. cm.

Summary: Skelly the skeleton girl finds a bone lying on the floor of her house and wonders where
it came from, and when she finally finds the answer, she is pleasantly surprised.

ISBN-13: 978-1-4169-1192-0

ISBN-10: 1-4169-1192-8

[1. Skeleton—Fiction. 2. Bones—Fiction. 3. Dogs—Fiction.]

I. Title.

PZ7.P55252Sk 2007

[E]—dc22

2006004023

first
edition

To Julian Chaney, the best pal this Skeleton Boy has ever had!

SKELLY
the Skeleton Girl

Written and illustrated by
JIMMY PICKERING

SIMON & SCHUSTER BOOKS FOR YOUNG READERS
New York   London   Toronto   Sydney

My name is

SKELLY.

I'm a skeleton girl.

This is my HOUSE, high on a hill.

I found a BONE
lying on my floor.

I asked my BAT
as we went for a stroll.

"No," he said.
"Does it belong to YOU?"

Could it be a BONE from me?
No, it wasn't mine.

X-RAY

I tickled the MONSTER
under the stairs, and he
started to LAUGH.

I knew he still had
his FUNNY BONE.

I asked my

MAN-EATING plants.

"No, my dear,
we wouldn't
eat THAT!"

I asked the GHOSTS who came to tea
if it belonged to them.

"Honey, we have no BONES."
"We lost those long ago."

I asked the SPIDER
who lived next door
if it could be his.

I checked my dolls from
HEAD to TOE. . . .
They hadn't lost
a STITCH.

This bony search was
making me HUNGRY.
I went to the kitchen
for a piece of CAKE.

past my
MAN-EATING plants,
into the
GARDEN.

I peeked around the TOPIARY HEDGE to see what the NOISE could be.

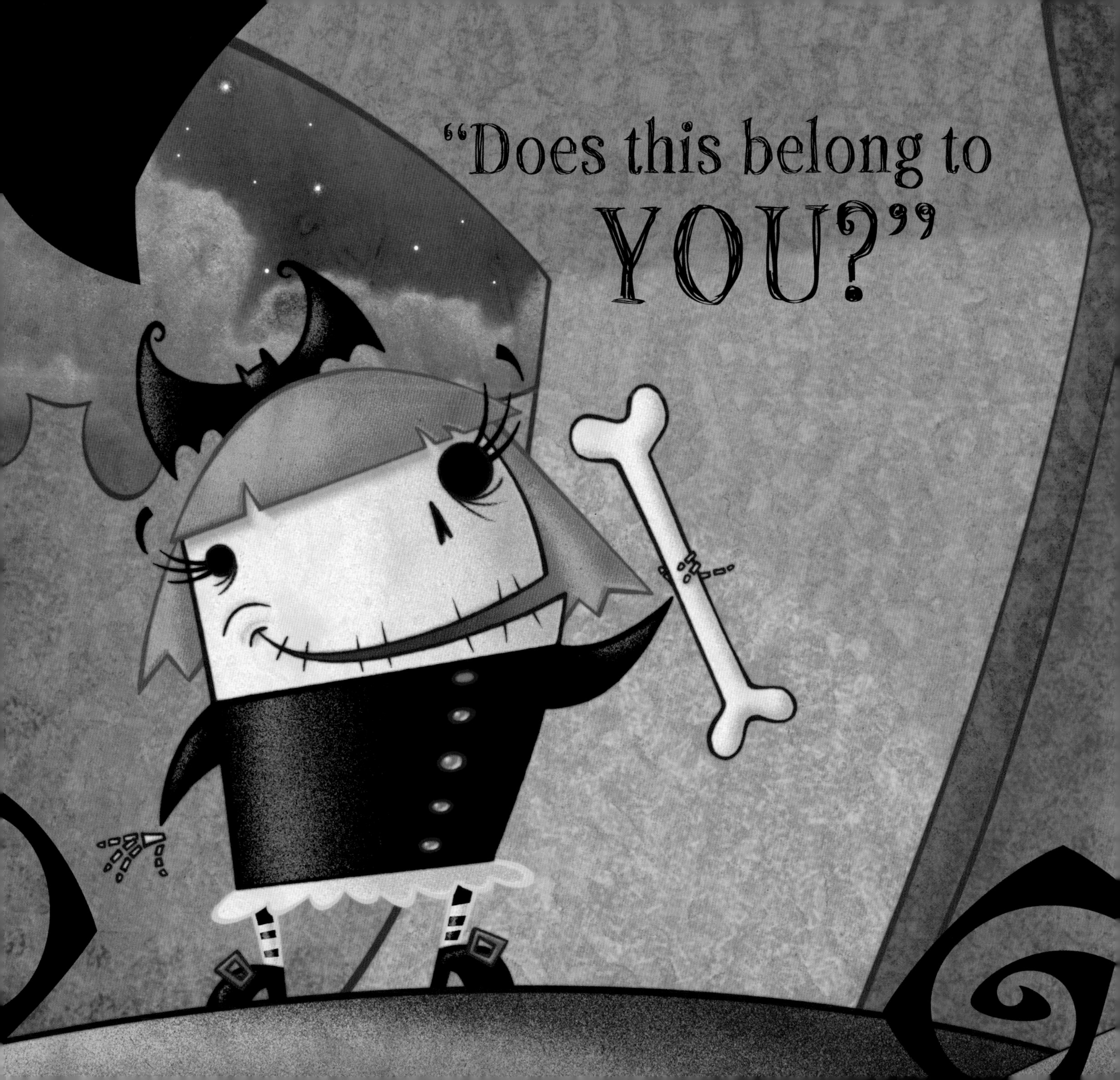

"Does this belong to
YOU?"

I found the owner of the BONE,
and I found a new
FRIEND, too!